This Walker book belongs to:

_____

_____

First published 1986
by Walker Books Ltd, 87 Vauxhall Walk, London SE11 5HJ

This edition published 2016

2 4 6 8 10 9 7 5 3 1

This book has been typeset in Bembo

Printed in China

British Library Cataloguing in Publication Data:
a catalogue record for this book is available from the British Library

ISBN 978-1-4063-7205-2

www.walker.co.uk

Smelly Jelly Smelly Fish
The Seaside Book

Michael Rosen   Quentin Blake

WALKER BOOKS
AND SUBSIDIARIES

LONDON · BOSTON · SYDNEY · AUCKLAND

On the Beach

There's a man over there
and he's sitting in the sand.
He buried himself at tea-time,
now he's looking for his hand.

There's a boy over there
and he's sitting on the rocks,
eating apple crumble,
washing dirty socks.

There's a woman over there
sitting in the sea.
I can see her
but she can't see me.

There's a girl over there
and she's sitting on a chair.
Standing just behind her
is a big grizzly bear.

Over My Toes

Over my toes
goes
the soft sea wash
see the sea wash
the soft sand slip
see the sea slip
the soft sand slide
see the sea slide
the soft sand slap
see the sea slap
the soft sand wash
over my toes.

What If...

What if
they made children-sized diggers
and you could take them down to the beach
to dig really big holes
and great big sandcastles
that the waves couldn't knock down.

What if
they made children-sized submarines
you could get into and go off underwater
looking at people's feet
and you could find old wrecked ships
and glide about
finding treasure.

What if
they made children-sized helicopters
that you took with you to the beach
so that you could take off in one of them
whenever you wanted to
and fly about above the beach
or up the cliffs
looking into those high-up caves
and swoop down again
towards the sea and some secret beach.

What if
they made children-sized ice creams…

Things We Say

Nat and Anna

Nat and Anna were walking along the beach.

Anna said, "You've got to look out for jellyfish, Nat."

Nat said, "I *am* looking out for jellyfish, Anna."

Anna said, "They're enormous."

Nat said, "I know they are."

Anna said, "And they're very yellow."

Nat said, "I know they are."

Anna said, "And they sting."

Nat said, "Oh."

Anna said, "They sting very hard and it really hurts."

Nat said, "Oh."

Nat started to walk very slowly and he was
looking at the sand very hard.

Anna said, "Come on, Nat. Keep up."

Nat said, "I am, Anna."

Anna said, "What's the matter, Nat?"

Nat said, "Nothing."

Anna said, "Are you worried about something, Nat?"

Nat said, "No."

Anna said, "Come on then."

Nat said, "Look out! That's a jellyfish, Anna! It's going to sting me, I want to go back! That's a jellyfish, Anna!"
Anna said, "Where?"
Nat said, "There!"
Anna said, "It's a piece of seaweed, Nat."

Nat went on walking very slowly,

looking at the sand very hard.

Anna said, "Stop there, Nat. Don't move."

Nat said, "I know. I can see it. I can see the jellyfish.

It's a really big one. It's going to sting me.

I want to go back, Anna."

Anna said, "Oh, it's flown away."

Nat said, "What's flown away?"

Anna said, "That seagull."

Nat said, "But *I'm* looking at the jellyfish. It's going to sting me! I want to go back, Anna! That's a jellyfish, Anna!"

Anna said, "Where?"

Nat said, "There!"

Anna said, "That's a piece of wood, Nat."

Nat went on walking very slowly.

Nat said, "Hey, Anna?"

Anna said, "Yes."

Nat said, "What's that?"

Anna screamed,

"*Yaaaaaaaaaaaaaaaaaaaaaaaaaaa!*"

Nat said, "What's the matter?"

Anna said, "That's a jellyfish. Don't touch it, Nat.
Don't go anywhere near it, Nat. It's a jellyfish."

Nat said, "Anna?"

Anna said, "Don't talk, Nat. Don't say anything."

Nat said, "Anna?"

Anna said, "Don't move, Nat. Don't move. It's going
to sting me. I want to go back. It's a jellyfish, Nat!"

Nat said, "Anna, it's an old balloon."

Anna looked at it for a long time.

Anna said, "So? So what if it is?"

Nat and Anna went very quiet.

Anna said, "Are you afraid of jellyfish, Nat?"

Nat said, "A bit."

Anna said, "Me too."

Nat said, "Smelly jellyfish."

Anna said, "Smelly jelly smelly fish."

Three Girls

There were three girls and they were going for
a walk along the beach till they came to a cave.
One of the girls says, "I'm going in."
So she goes in.

When she gets in, she sees a pile of gold
sitting on the rocks, so she thinks, "Yippee,
gold, all for me!" and she steps forward to
pick it up and a great big voice booms out,
"I'm the ghost of Captain Cox.
All the gold stays on the rocks."

So the girl runs out of the cave.

The second girl goes in and she sees the gold
and she thinks, "Yippee, gold, all for me!"
and she steps forward to pick it up and the
great big voice booms out,
"I'm the ghost of Captain Cox.
  All that gold stays on the rocks."

So the girl runs out of the cave.

Then the third girl goes in and she sees
the gold and she thinks, "Yippee, gold,
all for me!" and she steps forward to pick
it up and the great big voice goes,
"I'm the ghost of Captain Cox.
  All that gold stays on the rocks."
  And the girl says,
"I don't care. I'm the ghost of Davy Crocket
  and all that gold goes in my pocket!"
  and she runs out of the cave with the gold.

About the Author

Michael Rosen is one of the most popular authors of stories and poems for children. His titles include *We're Going on a Bear Hunt* (winner of the Smarties Book Prize), *Little Rabbit Foo Foo*, *Tiny Little Fly* and *Dear Mother Goose*. He has written many collections of poetry including *Let's Get Out of Here* and *Don't Put Mustard in the Custard*, both illustrated by Quentin Blake. He also compiled *Classic Poetry: An Illustrated Collection*. In 1997 he received the Eleanor Farjeon Award for services to children's literature and in 2007 he was appointed Children's Laureate.

About the Illustrator

Quentin Blake is a critically acclaimed children's book artist and was voted "The Illustrator's Illustrator" by *Observer* magazine. He is the illustrator of numerous Roald Dahl titles, several Michael Rosen poetry collections, *Michael Rosen's Sad Book* and *The Rights of the Reader* by Daniel Pennac. He has also created many acclaimed picture books of his own, including *Mr Magnolia* (winner of the Kate Greenaway Medal), *All Join In* (winner of the Kurt Maschler Award) and *Clown* (winner of Bologna Ragazzi Prize). In 1999 he was appointed the first Children's Laureate and in 2005 he was awarded a CBE for services to children's literature.